CW00847281

Mary Hooper knows more than most people what
makes a good story – she's had over six hundred
published in teenage and women's magazines such as
J17, and is the highly regarded author of over fifty
titles for young people, including *Best Friends, Worst
Luck*; *Mad About the Boy*; *The Boyfriend Trap*; and
the Letters to Liz series. She recently won the 2000
North-east Book Award for her teenage novel,
Megan. Mary has two grown-up children, Rowan and
Gemma, and lives in an old cottage in Hampshire.

Books by the same author

Jo's Letter
Nicki's Letter
Zoe's Letter
Best Friends, Worst Luck
The Boyfriend Trap
Mad About the Boy
The Peculiar Power of Tabitha Brown

Letters to Liz:
Amber's Letter

Mary Hooper

WALKER BOOKS
AND SUBSIDIARIES

LONDON • BOSTON • SYDNEY

First published 2002 by Walker Books Ltd
87 Vauxhall Walk, London SE11 5HJ

2 4 6 8 10 9 7 5 3 1

Text © 2002 Mary Hooper
Cover illustration © 2002 Rian Hughes
Cover design by Rian Hughes at Device

The right of Mary Hooper to be identified as author
of this work has been asserted by her in accordance
with the Copyright, Designs and Patents Act 1988

This book has been typeset in ITC Highlander Book

Printed and bound in Great Britain by The Guernsey Press Co. Ltd

British Library Cataloguing in Publication Data:
a catalogue record for this book
is available from the British Library

ISBN 0-7445-9004-3

Chapter One

It was the night I went to the cinema with my mates,
Zoe, Nicki and Jo, that I first suspected something
was going on. It was Friday and we'd been to the
multiplex in town to see this film about people
having affairs. It was supposed to be a comedy, and
basically everyone was copping off with everyone
else's boyfriend or girlfriend, husband or wife. None
of the relationships were what they seemed. The film
was OK, but not brilliant. The good thing was that
it hadn't cost us anything because Zoe's mum had

got us free tickets.

The four of us are really close friends and we go round together all the time. Sometimes – when one of us is going out with a boy and it's getting all smoochy – we don't see as much of each other as usual, but in the end it always comes back to us four: best friends for ever.

Mum was out when I got home from the cinema that night. This wasn't unusual for a Friday because she goes to a book group where they have long discussions about what they're reading. Afterwards they sometimes go on to a pub for a meal. Dad was home, though, because he was looking after my little brother Liam, who's seven. I've also got an older brother, Aidan, but he'd gone on a month-long course with his catering college.

Liam was in bed and Dad was in the sitting-room when I let myself in. Our front door is new and doesn't squeak when you open or close it, so although I said hello to Dad, the TV was on and he obviously hadn't heard me. I stood in the hall taking my jacket off and was just about to give Dad a yell when the music on the TV died down. I realized he was on the phone.

He was laughing – giggling, in fact. And this was rare. I mean, I have heard him giggle about things but not for ages. And certainly not with Mum. Bickering – yes. Giggling – no. And when he stopped giggling he said in a low voice, "Oh, you kill me, you know that?"

I hesitated outside the door for a moment, hearing him say that and thinking how strange it sounded. I mean, I couldn't think of anyone he would say that to. He just didn't have friends like that. And then almost immediately I started thinking about the film I'd just seen – the film about affairs. It was the sort of way they'd spoken to each other in that: in a joky, flattering, warm way.

I held my breath, listening.

"OK, Chicky," he went on. "Let's decide what time on Sunday and—"

But I'd heard enough. I was scared of what I'd hear next. Before he could say anything else I barged in. "Hi!" I said. "What's on telly?"

Chicky was the name he called me sometimes, and

called my little brother too, when he was in a good mood. Chicky meaning chicken, because he said we had browny-gold hair exactly the same colour as a chicken's feathers. But who was he calling that now?

Dad looked up, startled. "Amber! Just a sec," he said. He spoke into the receiver in a different voice. "See you soon, all right? Bye now!" He put the phone down.

"Who was that?" I asked.

"Bloke from work," he said. He kept his head down and didn't look at me. Rummaging through the newspapers on the floor he found that day's TV programmes. "Now, what have we got on next?" he muttered.

I stared at him. Bloke from work indeed! I didn't

believe him. You didn't call blokes from work Chicky. I thought about the film I'd just seen. Everyone had been at it in that – shop girls and office workers, teenagers and married women, the doctor and the secretary. They were all having affairs. And now – well, it seemed like my dad might be having one too.

I didn't sleep very well that night – I was too worried. Was he having an affair? Was it serious? What was going to happen next? Would he and Mum be getting a divorce? I wished there was someone I could tell. If Aidan had been home I could have talked to him about it, but he would be away for three more weeks.

*   *   *

The following morning my new copy of *Sue CQ*, the teen magazine, arrived, and I read it in bed, looking for features about people having affairs. Was it really as common as that film was trying to make out? Was everyone at it? How could you find out if they were?

I read the mag from cover to cover but I couldn't find anything about affairs, just the usual quizzes and fashion, and stuff about boy bands. There weren't even any problems about two-timing on the *Letters to Liz* problem pages.

I got up about eleven, still feeling worried, had a shower and went downstairs. Liam was riding his bike round and round the garden and Mum and Dad were eating bacon sandwiches in the kitchen. They were arguing, as usual. Dad was saying that he liked his bacon crispier and that the bread always went soggy the way *she* made sandwiches, and Mum was saying that if he was so bloody fussy he could make them himself.

I flopped down at the table, sighing loudly. "Give it a rest," I said. "Do you have to row every single day?"

Mum looked at me in surprise. "We're not rowing, Amber," she said, "just having a discussion."

"Sounds like a row to me," I said.

I stared at Dad. Did he look different? The men in the film all had new haircuts, shirts or shoes when they were having affairs. They'd started wearing aftershave and using new shampoos, and one had even had his hair tinted. Dad always looked pretty good, I thought. He didn't have a paunch, like most men his age, and he kept his hair nice and short and wore quite trendy clothes. At least he didn't wear patterned golfing jumpers like Nicki's dad.

"What are you staring at?" he suddenly asked me.

"Nothing!" I looked away and my glance fell on Mum. She looked a bit of a sight, actually. She was wearing jogging trousers and an old T-shirt of mine which had something spilt down the front. Her hair – which used to be goldie-brown like mine and my brother's – had been permed so many times it looked dry and straw-like.

Perhaps that was why Dad... But as soon as I thought that I pushed the idea away. Just because Mum had let herself go a bit didn't give Dad the right to have an affair. If he *was* having an affair.

I finished my cereal and Dad and Mum had coffee. Dad made it, then he said it tasted bitter and asked Mum if she'd bought the cheap brand. She said she'd bought the first ground coffee she'd seen – she didn't have time to pick and choose – but if he wanted to take over the shopping himself he was quite welcome … blah … blah … blah. And so it went on.

I was just about to get myself round to Jo's house – the four of us were meeting up and going shopping, as we usually did on a Saturday – when Dad said something about not being here the next day. He said he had to go into work to do the end-of-year accounts. Mum just shrugged as if she couldn't care less, but I looked at him suspiciously, remembering what he'd said on the phone the night before.

"Going to work on a *Sunday*?" I said. "I don't remember you ever doing that before."

"I've never been so behind with the accounts before," he said.

I fixed him with a look. I bet I know what you're up to, I thought...

Chapter Two

When Dad left the house the following morning I was peering at him through a crack in my bedroom curtains. What was he wearing? Did he look extra smart? Was he carrying anything suspicious?

As he drove off I went into the bathroom and looked round, sniffing. He'd used his new aftershave, and I could see from the tube of hair gel that he'd used that too. So he was obviously concerned about his appearance. But why? Who was going to see him at work on a Sunday?

I watched him disappear and wished that I could follow him. Was he *really* going to work?

Picking a book off my shelf, I went back to bed to read. It was still early and I didn't want Liam to know I was awake or he'd be in my room and bouncing all over me. What was going on with Dad? How could I find out?

I couldn't think of anything but him to start with, but the book I was reading was a funny one and by the end of two chapters I felt better. I decided that I had been jumping the gun as far as Dad was concerned. I'd only heard the tail-end of a phone call, after all – hardly caught him with a pair of knickers sticking out of his top pocket. And anyway, maybe he'd just been talking about work with one of the secretaries. He might call one of them Chicky.

I decided to give him the benefit of the doubt. I could have made some excuse to ring him at work that day to try and catch him out, but I decided not to. If he'd slipped out for a lunch-time pint or a sandwich and wasn't there – well, I'd worry all the more. No, I'd just stop thinking about it. At least until something else happened.

There wasn't anything suspicious about him when he came in that afternoon. In fact, he was back at four o'clock and he'd stopped off to buy a bunch of flowers for Mum at the station. They didn't seem to argue quite as much that evening either. So maybe it was all OK, I thought.

*   *   *

Until Wednesday, that was. It was early evening and the four of us were round at Zoe's house, playing garage full volume. Her mum was out and even though her house is detached we were making such a racket that one of the neighbours banged on the door to complain.

Zoe cheeked him, and turned the music up louder, and then he came back to say that if she didn't stop the noise he was going to call the police. Course, she didn't want this, so we decided to quit the house pretty quickly.

"I'll give him one good loud blast," she said, "and then we'll slip out the back. With a bit of luck he'll call the police and they'll arrive to find no one home and everything quiet."

"That'll teach him," I said.

"Won't someone tell your mum, though?" Nicki asked. "My mum would go absolutely ballistic if one of the neighbours called the police."

Zoe shrugged, tossing back her long blonde hair. "He's got to find her in first," she said.

She set her CD to play one last track and then we were out the back within seconds, giggling our way down the road.

"Where are we going?" I asked, and one by one we all gave reasons why we couldn't go back to our houses. It was only Zoe, actually, who had a bedroom big and comfortable enough for four girls to sprawl in.

"It'll have to be the square, then," Nicki said. The square is a big open space in town where groups of kids meet up. "And it's Wednesday," she added. "We might get the boys from Marsham Grammar there."

We all perked up at the thought of the Marsham boys. We knew that a crowd of them went to footie practice on a Wednesday and often hung around the square afterwards.

"Wish I'd worn my new trainers!" Nicki wailed.

"It'll be dark by the time we get there," Zoe said. "No one will be able to see your feet."

"*I'll* be able to see them," Nicki said, while I remembered that I hadn't even got the tiniest bit of eye make-up on. My eyelashes are light and gingery, and without mascara or anything I look like a pale pink pig. I shrugged to myself: too bad.

On the way down there something happened that

wiped all thoughts of mascara from my mind.

We'd caught the bus in and were just about to cross the zebra crossing to the square. A van stopped for us and then, just behind that, a car was waiting. It was a dark green Rover, like my dad's and about a million others, but something – God knows what – made me look at it more closely. With a small, cold shock I realized that my dad was in the driver's seat – but it wasn't my mum next to him.

For just two seconds I stopped dead, taking it in, and then I pulled myself together and went after the others. Dad hadn't seen me: he and the woman were looking at each other and laughing. She was younger than Mum – smaller, with short curly hair.

I reached the square on the other side, the van

and car passed us, and I caught up with the others.

"What's up, Amber?" Jo asked me, but I just shook my head.

Dad hadn't said he was going out. In fact, he and Mum were settling down to watch TV when I left and had already started the usual bicker about who was going to hold the remote control. It was him, though. I was sure of it. I was ninety-nine per cent sure.

I felt like going home immediately to check on him. If he was there it would all be all right.

But I didn't go. I didn't want to drag all the way back on the bus when I'd only just got there and anyway, Zoe and co. would have thought it was strange. The Marsham boys were in the square and I spent an hour or so chatting to them and pretending to be interested in the finer points of football. I think the others enjoyed themselves there – anywhere with boys is good for Zoe and Nicki – but I didn't.

I couldn't remember a thing about the offside rule by the time I walked back to my house. All I could see was that Dad's car wasn't in the drive.

I shouted that I was home, then went into the sitting-room and looked round casually. "No Dad?" I asked. "Where is he?"

Mum hardly looked up from the new doctors series she was watching. "Oh, he had to go out, love. Got a call from work. Sit down and watch the last bit of this. It's brilliant!"

I slid down onto the sofa beside her, my heart

thumping. My one last hope had been that he'd be home, and that I'd just seen someone who looked a lot like him, in the same sort of car.

But no. It *must* have been him. So he was definitely having an affair...

Chapter Three

I lay awake practically all night wondering what to
do. Who was the woman? How long had it been
going on? Was it serious? What would Mum do when
she heard — and should I be the one to tell her? The
questions went round and round in my head and
none of them had any answers. I'd never had to deal
with anything as serious as this before and I just
didn't know what to do for the best. If Aidan was
here I would have asked him what to do, but as he
wasn't, I had to find someone else...

At school the next day, after we'd had our lunch, I told the others I had to go and do something in the library.

"Get you!" said Zoe. "What have you got to do that's so much more important than chatting to your mates?"

"Oh, I've just got a couple of letters to write about work experience," I lied. "I want to use the computers."

"Use mine at home," Zoe said. She had one of those cool purple iMacs.

I shook my head. "Nah," I said. "Can't concentrate with you lot around."

I left them sitting on the field, went to one of the library computers, got a new file started and began my letter. Only it wasn't to any work experience place – I was writing to Liz, the agony aunt in *Sue CQ*.

Dear Liz,

There's something really awful happening at home and I don't know what to do. I think my dad is having an affair. That is, I'm sure he is having an affair. I have actually seen him out with the woman. I don't know how long it's been going on for or anything.

What do you think I should do? Should I tell my mum? What do you think is going to happen to me and my brothers? If they get a divorce will we have to go into a children's home or might we have to be fostered? I read about someone whose mum got a divorce and neither parent really wanted her so she had to go to a foster home and live with about ten kids that no one wanted. I would hate that. I'd run away rather than have that happen. Please tell me what to do.

Don't write to me at home in case my mum sees the letter and wonders who it's from. I'll look for your answer on the Dear Liz page.

Yours sincerely,

A Leonardo DiCaprio fan

I went through it a couple of times, changing things and making it sound better, then printed it out. I got an envelope and looked in *Sue CQ* for the address, and then noticed that it said you should allow eight weeks for your problem to be printed and they couldn't guarantee to print every letter they got.

Which was absolutely no good to me at all. I wanted some help and I wanted it now.

Downstairs in the school cloakroom, I tore the letter into bits and flushed it down the loo. I had no one to help me and no one to tell. What was I going to do?

For a day or two after that I watched Dad all the time. I found myself spying on him, looking at his clothes, sniffing around him for strange perfumes – even examining his shirts to see if there were any traces of lipstick. No suspicious wife could have searched more thoroughly than I did. I was looking for evidence, and once I had that, I could confront him.

Or, I worried endlessly, *should* I confront him? Wouldn't it be better to tell Mum, so she could do it? What was the right thing to do?

If it had been anything else – like problems with periods, or boys, or school – I would have asked my mates. For some reason, though, I couldn't bring myself to say a word to them about what was happening with Mum and Dad. I guess I was too scared of what they might say – that yeah, my mum and dad were definitely heading for divorce and the family would be split up and we'd all have to go and live in a horrible bed and breakfast place or something.

It all seemed too serious to tell them. Other problems – well, no matter how badly you'd had your heart broken by some boy or other, or how much you hated a teacher at school, deep down you knew that you'd get over it, and if you told Zoe and co. you knew that in the end you'd be able to laugh about it. This, though – *divorce* – was real grown-up stuff. It seemed to me the most serious and horrible thing that could ever happen.

On Thursday I was late getting home from school because I'd got into the netball team and we had to practise, so Dad was in before me. Mum was upstairs helping Liam with his homework, so I thought I'd sound Dad out. I just wanted to see how he felt about certain things.

He was sitting at the kitchen table reading the

sports pages of the paper, and I made myself a cup of tea and just sat down and started chatting. I pretended there was a girl at school whose mum and dad were breaking up.

"It's really awful," I said. "Sammy's mum's left her dad and gone to live in Australia. She's left Sammy and her sister behind!"

"Yeah – sad, that," Dad said, shaking his head. "It happens, though, doesn't it."

"But it shouldn't," I said. "People should be faithful for life."

"What – like swans?" Dad said, chuckling.

I glowered at him. "I don't know how you can laugh," I said. "Poor Sammy's heartbroken. It's ruined her life!"

Dad shrugged. "Well, I'm sorry for Sammy," he said, "but there's not a lot I can do. Who's Sammy, anyway? I've never heard you talk about her before. Why are you so worried about her?"

"She's just a friend from school," I said, going red. "And I'm only telling you because ... because I just thought I would," I finished lamely.

I drank the rest of my tea and went upstairs. He hadn't seemed particularly embarrassed or wary; I hadn't found out anything one way or the other.

I'd keep watching and waiting, I decided, until the weekend. He'd be bound to want to see her and then I'd make a move. I'd try and follow him and confront him, or I'd tell Mum...

Chapter Four

On Saturday, when I went downstairs, Dad was
outside cleaning the car.

"Dad's up and about early," I said to Mum casually.
"Is he going out somewhere?"

"Don't think so," Mum said. She was standing
by the cooker – we always had a proper cooked
breakfast at weekends. "Not that he's mentioned
to me, anyway."

"Has he got to work again tomorrow?"

Mum shook her head, then she went to the door

and yelled to Dad that his breakfast was getting cold. "He knew I was just about to start cooking," she grumbled.

Liam was at the table finishing off a plate of scrambled eggs. He pulled a face at me as I sat down, but for once I didn't pull one back. I felt sorry for him. If our parents were splitting up, that would mean he'd only had seven years in a normal family. The rest of his childhood would be spent being shuffled backwards and forwards between Mum and Dad, not knowing where he belonged.

Tug of love. I'd seen it in the papers only that week – a dad who'd kidnapped his son and taken him abroad so that his wife wouldn't get to keep him. It wouldn't happen to me – I could decide for myself who I was going to live with — but Liam might be fought over and wouldn't have a say in what happened.

I started to think about who I'd live with, given a choice. It was a hard one. I mean, Mum and Dad both drove me mad sometimes but I didn't want to be without either of them, long-term. How could I possibly choose between them? What would the other one, the one I rejected, feel like? And anyway, suppose Dad made a home with this new woman — would she want me there? Maybe no one would want me and I'd have to go into a foster home. Maybe Dad would take the two boys, and Mum would have me, and I'd only see my brothers once a year—

"Amber!" Mum said, exasperated. "I think you're still half asleep. I've asked you three times if you want mushrooms with your bacon."

"Yeah. Sorry, I was thinking of something else," I said.

"Thinking of going deaf," Liam said. Getting up, he pulled another – even more horrible – face at me.

But I didn't pull a face or say anything rude back. If the family was splitting up, he and I would have to stick together.

That afternoon, I met up with the other three to go shopping. I didn't really want to go. I mean, I suppose a bit of me wanted to get out of the house, but the other bit wanted to stay and spy. I needed to know for sure one way or the other what was happening, and when it was happening. If Dad was going to go off and leave us and I wasn't going to have a home, then I wanted to know the very worst as soon as possible.

Of course, this meant I was preoccupied and couldn't concentrate on the task in hand, which was to find Zoe something special to wear for a party at one of her mum's posh clients'. Her mum had given her a blank cheque and she was allowed to buy whatever she wanted, as long as she looked "stylish but not tarty" as her mum put it.

The three of us hangers-on – well, our tongues were hanging out in envy at the stuff Zoe tried on. It was real designer gear, all the top labels. We sat squashed into a fitting room, giggling and making comments, as Zoe went through half the stuff in Kelly-Marie's.

I watched her, thinking that *she* didn't have a dad around and it didn't seem to affect her much. As long as I'd known her she'd only ever had her mum; she'd never spoken about a dad.

"That's the one!" Nicki said. Zoe had narrowed her choice down to a shortlist of three outfits and was wearing the second of these. It was a scarlet dress made of beautiful fabric, cut on the cross so it waved gently around Zoe's calves. With her long blonde hair and the tan she had, it looked sensational.

"You look like a pop star," Jo said in a gushy voice, and we all screeched with laughter.

Going home, I managed to sit on the bus next to Zoe. There was something I really wanted to ask her.

"You know your dad..." I began.

She looked at me blankly. "No."

"Well, you must have ... I mean, didn't you ever have a dad living with you?"

She shook her head. "My mum says she wanted a baby so she called up a friend."

"So the friend is your dad?"

"Sort of. Not exactly a dad, though. My mum doesn't see him now. They're not friends any more."

"But isn't it funny not having anyone – not having a man around the place?"

"No," Zoe said again, looking at me a bit scornfully. "I haven't even got a mum half the time because she's always out." She shrugged. "Anyway, I've got used to it. What you've never had, you don't miss."

I thought about what she'd said and decided she was probably right. I *had* had a dad, though. And I *would* miss him.

When I got back from shopping, Mum and Dad were both out – together, I presumed – and Liam was with them.

I went into the sitting-room and looked round. It seemed weird – unbelievable, actually – to think that soon I might not be living there. I knew that usually when divorces happened the family home had to be sold.

How could he do it? I felt like I hated him for putting me through all this. It seemed as if everything I knew, my whole life, was about to be turned on its head.

Suddenly I noticed Dad's briefcase standing in a corner of the sitting-room, by his chair. Maybe I'd be able to find some real hard evidence in there! It had a combination lock, but I knew the number. It was my birth date and my brothers' birth dates: 23147.

I went over and picked up the briefcase, keeping one eye on the drive in case our car drew up. I didn't feel in the slightest bit guilty. It was Dad's fault: if he'd been faithful to Mum then I wouldn't be doing this.

I opened the case and flicked briefly through the loose papers inside, then looked into a plastic folder.

Nothing interesting. I found his Filofax and quickly looked through it to see if I could see any strange women's names and telephone numbers, but with no luck. Looking in the back pocket of the Filofax, though, I found a wodge of papers: petrol receipts, notes about DIY stuff, invoices folded in half.

And right in the middle of all these I found exactly the sort of thing I'd been looking for. It was a receipt, folded very small, and when I opened it out I saw that it was a bill for a "gourmet meal" for two and a bottle of champagne at Clementine's, a French restaurant, on May 11th this year.

May 11th. For some reason this date rang a bell — and suddenly I remembered why. That night had been a special parents' evening for our class. All our parents had been invited to see the work we'd done during the year and to talk about what exams we were going to do. It was a very important evening (our teachers had emphasized this). They'd said that what was decided that evening could affect our futures.

Dad hadn't come, and I remembered the reason he'd given: he'd had to fly to Scotland to meet an important client. I looked at the address at the top of the restaurant bill. Not Scotland, but Yardley, a town about twenty miles away.

He hadn't been in Scotland at all. He'd been in Clementine's, with the woman he was having the affair with.

Chapter Five

Carefully, I folded the receipt just the way I'd found it, put it back in the Filofax and locked the briefcase.

My dad was just the same as all the dodgy characters in that film. He was a love rat! He'd been unfaithful. Had a mistress. Had cheated on my mum. Was an adulterer. Had slept around.

All the different ways of saying it went through my head, yet I still couldn't believe it. *Not my dad*. It felt as if I'd found out he was a murderer.

It was true, though. Of course it was. And really,

not only was he being unfaithful to Mum, he was being unfaithful to me too – putting me last, not coming to my school open evening because he'd rather be with her, his mistress. The two of them had had a gourmet meal – whatever that was. And a bottle of champagne.

And to think that he was so mean about spending money on eating out with us! A pub steak and chips was about as extravagant as he got – but *she* got French meals and champagne...

I seethed for an hour or so, until they came in, and then I made a point of glowering at Dad, turning on my heel and going straight upstairs. I wasn't going to sit and watch the usual Saturday evening stuff on TV with them. Certainly not.

"What's up with her?" I heard him ask Mum.

"Haven't a clue," Mum said.

On Monday I asked Mum if she'd ever been to Clementine's. I wanted to make perfectly sure that it wasn't her who'd been there with him – maybe the restaurant had got the date on the receipt wrong or something.

I knew the answer already, though. I mean, if they'd been anywhere like that, for an anniversary or something, I would have heard about it.

"What's Clementine's?" she asked. She'd just come back from the supermarket and was unpacking a ton of food.

"A French restaurant," I said. "In Yardley."

"Ha!" she said. "Who's going to take me to a French restaurant?" I didn't say anything and she added, "What d'you want to know for, anyway?"

"Oh, I ... Zoe's mum takes her clients there," I lied. "It sounds really posh. I just wondered if you'd been."

"No, but I think I'd like to."

"Zoe's mum goes to all sorts of places," I said. "She's been to New York masses of times."

Mum sighed. "Lucky old Zoe's mum," she said. "And what's good about her is that she's got where she is without the aid of a man."

"But you ... you wouldn't want to be without Dad, would you?" I asked.

"Sometimes," Mum said darkly. And then she laughed. "Only joking."

*   *   *

That evening someone phoned for Dad. It was about eight o'clock and he'd already said that he was going out later – "For a drink down the pub with a couple of chaps from the golf course," he'd told us.

I took the call, because I was just coming down the stairs on my way out to Jo's house. It was a woman's voice, quite softly spoken.

"Can I speak to Alan?" she said, and I was immediately on guard.

"I'm not sure if he's in," I said – though I knew he was in the sitting-room watching *EastEnders*. "Who's calling, please?"

"It's Diane," she said, and added, "from work."

I bet! I thought. It was on the tip of my tongue to

say he wasn't in, but I didn't quite have the nerve for that, just in case it was on the level. Instead I decided to hang around and put him off his stride.

I put the receiver down and went to the sitting-room door. "It's someone called Diane," I announced.

Mum didn't look up — but Dad certainly did. "For me?" he said, startled.

I nodded. "Diane from work — *she said*," I added in an undertone as he went by me.

He went into the hall and picked up the receiver, while I just stood there staring at him.

He turned his back on me. "Yes?" he asked.

I didn't hear what she said but after a moment Dad said quite bluntly, "Well, it can't be helped. Not to worry. Some other time." That was all. And then he put the phone down.

He looked at me. "What are you hanging about for?"

"Who's Diane?" I asked. "One of the secretaries?"

"Nothing to do with you!" he said, in a falsely jolly voice. "Anyway, I thought you were going out."

"I am," I said, and then I thought I'd test him. "Can you give me a lift round to Jo's house on your way to the pub?"

"Who said I was going to the pub?"

"You did. Earlier."

He went back into the sitting-room. "I changed my mind," he said over his shoulder. "There are some good programmes on TV tonight."

I just stood there, staring at his back. Of course! She'd cancelled their date – she couldn't get out for some reason. Maybe she was married as well. And so now he wasn't meeting his "golf mates".

It all seemed to be coming to a head. She had the nerve to ring here now and it only needed for Mum to put two and two together. She was bound to find out soon. And *then* the fireworks would begin...

Chapter Six

I badly wanted Aidan to come back so that I could talk to someone about what was going on. I mean, Aidan was the only person – not counting Mum – who would know exactly how I felt and who had as much to lose as I did.

When I got round to Jo's that evening, Zoe and Nicki were there too, of course. They were going on about Chris, this boy they both fancied, and pretending to have a mock auction for him, while Jo and I did a quiz in *Sue CQ*. Then we looked through some back issues and found some stuff about a girls'-night-in beauty spa. We decided to have one of these the following week and Zoe volunteered to bring everything she could from her mum's collection of lotions and potions.

"She's got everything!" she said. "She picks up caseloads of stuff when she stays in hotels. I bet she's got everything we need."

"That's good," Nicki said. She looked at Zoe. "Doesn't your mum ever get fed up with travelling around?"

Zoe shook her head. "She loves it. She said once that if it wasn't for me she'd be on the road all the time."

I looked thoughtfully at Zoe. She'd told me it was

all right without a dad — and half the time she didn't have a mum around either. So maybe you *could* survive.

But I didn't *want* to just survive...

Tears came into my eyes and I blinked them back. I didn't want the others to see and ask what was up — I just didn't feel I could tell them.

The evening went on and then me, Zoe and Nicki got ready to go home. The two of them were going to walk back together because they wanted to go the long way, past Chris's house, to see if they could spot him. I was set to leave too, but in the opposite direction, so Jo said if I hung on a couple of minutes she'd walk down the road with me.

As soon as Zoe and Nicki had gone Jo said, "I only

asked you to stay back because you looked really upset earlier. I thought you were going to cry. I wanted to ask you what was up."

Course, as soon as she spoke to me sympathetically I burst into tears and began crying and crying. It felt as if all my tears had been building up and I'd just been waiting for someone to turn the tap on.

She sat patiently, patting my shoulder and handing me tissues. "What's up, then?" she asked when I'd finally managed to stop and blow my nose. "It's not some guy messing you around, is it?"

I shook my head.

"I thought not," she said. "If it was, you'd have told us. That means it's either something at school – but I think you would have told us that too – or about your family."

I nodded and sniffed. "I couldn't say anything before because I just felt so ..." I struggled helplessly for the right word, "so sort of embarrassed, I suppose. What it is, is that ... I think my dad's having an affair," I said in a rush, relieved to have told someone at last.

"Oh!" she said with a little gasp. "Are you sure?"

I nodded. "I've seen him with her, and there's been phone calls and stuff."

"Does your mum know?"

I shook my head. "D'you think I should tell her?"

"No," Jo said. "Look, I'll tell you something. Two years ago, my *mum* had an affair."

"No!" I said, startled. "You never told us."

"I know." She gave a rueful grin. "It wasn't

something that I wanted to announce. I felt like you – embarrassed and ashamed, really."

"What happened? She obviously didn't go off with him."

Jo shook her head. "For a while, though, I thought she would. He was American and I had visions of her going away and leaving me and my sister behind. I thought we'd have to go into a children's home."

I stared at her. "That's just what I've been thinking."

She shook her head. "That won't happen," she said. "Think about your mum and dad. D'you really think either of them would just go off and leave you? Put you in a home?"

I shrugged. "I dunno. I guess not."

"Look, I got so upset when it was all going on that my mum sent me to talk to some counsellor woman. She told me that my parents loved me and would continue to love me, and I was to try and keep out of what was going on. She said that it was just between them, and also that I wasn't to blame my mum – that I had no idea of the pressures inside a marriage. She said when someone has an affair it's just a symptom that something else is wrong."

I sat listening, trying to take all this in.

"She also said I had no idea of the circumstances – that for all she or I knew my dad might have had an affair first."

"Oh," I said. I couldn't imagine my mum ... but then I couldn't imagine my dad either.

"The main thing *you* have to do is keep your head down and let them work things out for themselves. It's not your problem – it's theirs."

"But what happened with your mum?" I asked.

"Well, she did split up from my dad," Jo said, "and he went to live with a friend – but only for a couple of months. My mum carried on seeing the American man, and then one day she and my dad got together to talk about things and in the end she asked him to come back home."

"And then what happened?"

"Well, it's not exactly been happy ever after," Jo said, shrugging. "I hear them arguing sometimes when I've gone to bed. But, well, I dunno. Maybe that's normal."

"So you don't think I ought to tell my mum what I've found out?"

Jo shook her head. "No, I don't. You could hint to your dad that you know, though. That might make him bring things to a head. I don't know about you, but I found the waiting, the not knowing what's going to happen, the worst bit."

I nodded. "It is," I said. I sat for some moments, thinking over what Jo had said. It seemed to make sense. It was the sort of thing that Liz told the girls who wrote to her: that it was their parents' problem, not theirs.

"Thanks, Jo," I said shakily.

"That's OK," she said. "It's easy to help when you've been through it all yourself." She put an arm round my shoulders. "It'll probably be all right."

"But if not..."

"If not, then I'll be around if you want another dollop of advice."

"Thanks," I said again.

I suddenly felt a lot better. It was just such a relief to get it all out and talk about it. And as Jo said, it would probably be all right in the end. I really hoped so. I guessed I just had to leave my mum and dad to find that out for themselves, though.

Find out what Amber, Jo, Nicki and Zoe get up to

in another book from the Letters to Liz series:

Zoe's Letter

(Turn the page to read the first chapter.)

Chapter One

Dear Liz,

I've never written to an agony aunt before. In fact,
I've always thought that people who write to magazines
with their problems are pretty sad. This is something
that I just can't tell my friends, though. It's a really big
problem and it seems to have taken over my life. It's
about a boy. Of course, it mostly is when girls are
writing to you, but I'll tell you now that it's not like me
to get so hooked on a boy that I can't think straight.

It all started two nights ago, at the skating rink...

I put down my pen and closed my eyes. I was going to write the letter in rough first, and then type it out afterwards, but I wanted to sort things out in my head before I started.

We – me, Amber, Jo and Nicki – had gone skating, just for something to do, really. The four of us are really good friends. We've been going round together for ages now, since about the second year of primary school, although my mum was all set to break us up when I was twelve because she didn't want me to go on to the local comprehensive with them. She's a bit like that – a real snob – and she was going to send me off to some posh boarding school. I kicked up a fuss about leaving the others, though – said I would run away – and in the end she gave in and let me stay.

Anyway, we'd decided to go ice-skating, just to make a change from drinking Cokes in Beany's or going down the square to see who was hanging out. Also, Jo had got these vouchers that gave two-for-one entry to the rink, so we thought we might as well give it a go.

We didn't go down there to try and meet boys, but if there were any around that we hadn't seen before (you can always hope) then that would be a bonus. Mind you, Amber wasn't really interested in meeting anyone, because she had Mac. Mac has recently come to our school from Scotland. He's well fit, with a gorgeous body and a Highlander accent so strong you could cut porridge with it. At first we'd laughed at the way he spoke, and the boys had taken the mick out of him, but actually all of us girls reckoned his accent was gorgeous. I could have listened to it all day.

So anyway, we got to the rink, hired our skates and sat around lacing them up, trying on each other's and changing them at the counter until we were satisfied they fitted OK. We were a bit giggly and nervous. I mean, we'd all been roller-blading before so we weren't going to be totally useless, but no one likes to look a complete dork, do they?

It was the first time I'd been ice-skating there – it was sort of old-fashioned with funny big globe lights and glittery disco balls. The rink itself was huge and echoey, and a frosty sort of mist hung over the ice.

We pulled each other round, pushed each other over and shrieked and giggled as we went round the rink a few times, mostly holding onto the edge. Then we hobbled along to the bar, still on our blades, to get a Coke.

We started talking about boys, of course, and whether there was anyone there we liked the look of. Jo, who isn't usually into boys as much as the rest of us, said she really fancied the guy who'd given out the boots, and Amber said she couldn't think about anyone else because she was completely mad about Mac. She said she was never going to fancy anyone else as long as she lived.

Course, we all screeched with laughter at this.

"I *won't*," Amber said. She's got red-gold hair and she tucked a strand of it behind one ear and squeezed her eyes up tightly. "He's so ... so utterly gorgeous in every way."

"He's just a bloke!" I said. "How can he be?"

The other two laughed but Amber was quite insistent. "If you knew him like I do you'd think the same," she said. "He's got a way of really listening to you. He's so understanding. He always wants to know what I've been doing and what I think about and all that. And he's thoughtful."

"Thoughtful?" I said. "That's a new one!"

"I've never heard any of the blokes we've been out with called thoughtful before," Nicki said.

"Exactly," Amber went on. "Mac really likes girls. He knows what makes them tick."

Well, we all laughed again but it got me thinking. Why couldn't I get a boy like that? Someone *thoughtful.* Someone who knew how to treat a girl. The ones I got were usually good-looking, flash jack-the-lads, and could never be called thoughtful by any stretch of the imagination. And if they were, it was only for one reason. Like they'd "thoughtfully" ask you round to their house to copy a CD for you, and then you'd find it just so happened that their parents were out, and then they'd "thoughtfully" ask you if you wanted to watch a video, and they'd "thoughtfully" turn the lights down, and – well, you get the picture.

We all finished our drinks and then went back on the rink. Holding onto each other and grabbing at the sides for support, we actually managed to go round a few times without falling over.

We sat down again and Nicki said she'd twisted her ankle a bit. We were just discussing whether we could manage another drink or should just go home, when there was a "Hey!" from the other side of the rink and who should appear but Mac, waving wildly at us. He was with Sam, a boy I'd gone out with a couple of times in the distant past.

They came onto the ice and speed-skated over, curling round to a halt in front of us in the way that boys do, spraying up ice.

"Not bad!" Amber said. She was so happy to see him. I thought to myself that when she'd packed in her last boyfriend – some creep called Jamie – it was the best thing she'd ever done.

"I practised in the Highlands," Mac said. "You can

skate down mountains there."

"You come from Glasgow," I said. "They haven't got mountains."

"OK then," he grinned at me. "It's just my natural grace and skill."

"Yeah, right," I said.

Sam spoke up. "So you got the half-price vouchers too?"

We all nodded.

"We've been here an hour or so. My feet are freezing!" Amber said. "We were just thinking about going home."

"Och, do a couple of rounds with me before you go," Mac said.

Amber started pulling her gloves on again.

"OK. But promise you won't go too fast?"

"Would I do that?"

He led her off onto the ice and Sam took Jo for a spin round at the same time. I'd had enough, really, so I said I'd sit with Nicki while she wiggled her ankle to get it back to normal.

I watched Mac and Amber on the ice; he had his arm around her, pulling her close, and every so often she'd laugh up at him or give a squeal of enjoyment. Lucky old Amber, I thought, to have that sort of a relationship with someone. I had a boyfriend too – a guy called Paul who was in the year above us – but it wasn't going anywhere. He was just someone to hang around with, like everyone else I'd ever been out with, really.

Mac and Amber went round the rink twice and

then she arrived, puffing, back beside me. "It's much better when you're with someone who knows what they're doing," she said. "It was really good fun."

Mac looked at me and held out his hand. "Want some of that really good fun, Zoe?" he said in his gorgeous accent, and for a moment I just sat there, staring up at him, struck dumb and feeling sort of hypnotized.

That's really odd for me, because – well, I'm not being big-headed but I've got very long blonde hair and I got boobs quite early on, so I've never exactly been hard-up for boys. They're like buses, I always say – there'll be another one along in a minute.

When Mac said that, though, and looked at me, I felt a shiver run all over me. Why hadn't I noticed him before? This guy was something else...

So, we just went around the rink together and had a laugh, but for the rest of the evening I just felt like I was in a sort of trance. All I could think of, all I could see, was Mac. He was all around me, all over me ... I could still feel his fingers on my arm.

I picked up my pen again — I hadn't got very far with the letter.

Liz, nothing happened except he looked at me, spoke my name and took me once around the ice rink, but it's just made me feel absolutely weird. I can't stop thinking about him...

I put the pad away. Thinking was OK, but trying to

write the things that I felt was too difficult. How could you translate feelings into words?

Mac. I conjured him up in my head, and tried saying my name aloud the way he said it: it sounded like Zoo-ey.

Mac. I was mad about him. And he was going out with Amber.